For Angela and Edgar
—B. B.

For Marcus, Zac, and Jason—
supreme partners in my own imaginary days
—E. B.

Henry Holt and Company, LLC, *Publishers since 1866*
175 Fifth Avenue, New York, New York 10010
www.henryholtchildrensbooks.com

Henry Holt® is a registered trademark of Henry Holt and Company, LLC.
Text copyright © 2006 by Betsy Byars
Illustrations copyright © 2006 by Erik Brooks
All rights reserved. Distributed in Canada by H. B. Fenn and Company Ltd.

Library of Congress Cataloging-in-Publication Data
Byars, Betsy Cromer.
Boo's dinosaur / Betsy Byars; illustrated by Erik Brooks.—1st ed.
p. cm.
"An early chapter book."
Summary: When young Boo is followed home by a dinosaur that only
she can see, it causes a bit of trouble for her older brother, Sammy.
ISBN-13: 978-0-8050-7958-6 / ISBN-10: 0-8050-7958-0
[1. Imagination—Fiction. 2. Brothers and sisters—Fiction. 3. Dinosaurs—Fiction.]
I. Brooks, Erik, ill. II. Title.
PZ7.B9836Boo 2006   [E]—dc22   2006000726

First Edition—2006 / Designed by Patrick Collins
Printed in the United States of America on acid-free paper. ∞

1 3 5 7 9 10 8 6 4 2

Contents

1. Boo Plays Dinosaurs   1
2. Boo's Dinosaur   8
3. Boo's Book   16
4. Boo Jumps on the Bed   24
5. Boo High up a Tree   30
6. Boo and the Magic Cape   36

1
Boo Plays Dinosaurs

"Let's play dinosaurs," Boo said to her brother. "You can be this dinosaur. I will be this one."

Sammy said, "Don't bother me. I am reading a book."

Boo said, "My dinosaur is eating leaves. What is your dinosaur doing?"

Sammy said, "Don't bother me. I am reading a book."

"My dinosaur is swimming," Boo said. "What is your dinosaur doing?"

Sammy said, "Don't bother me. I am reading a book."

"Play! Come on! Let's play! Please, please, please, please, *please.*"

"Oh, all right," Sammy said. "My dinosaur is playing ball."

Boo said, "That is not fair. Dinosaurs don't play ball."

"Oh, all right," Sammy said. "My dinosaur is listening to a story."

"Dinosaurs do not—" Boo began, then she stopped. She asked, "Can my dinosaur listen, too?"

"Yes," Sammy said.

Sammy read the story.

Boo said, "I wish I had a real dinosaur." She got up. "I'm going out and find one."

Sammy said, "Find me one, too."

"I'll try," said Boo.

2
Boo's Dinosaur

Boo came back in a hurry.

"Mom, an animal followed me home. Can I keep it?" she asked. "Please, please, please, please, *please!*"

Mom asked, "Is it a dog?"

Boo said, "No."

Mom asked, "Is it a cat?"

Boo said, "No."

Dad looked up from his book. "Is it a croc?" he asked.

Boo said, "No."

"Is it a dragon?"

"No, but you are getting close," Boo said.

Sammy said, "It is a dinosaur."

"*Yes! Yes!* How did you know?" Boo asked.

"Is this one of those animals that nobody can see but you?" Dad asked.

"No, it is a real live dinosaur. Come, I'll show you."

Dad and Boo went to the window.

Boo said, "There!"

Dad looked this way. He looked that way. "Yes, you can keep it," he said.

Boo said, "Thank you, thank you, *thank you!* All my life I have wanted a dinosaur and now one has followed me home. I am the luckiest girl in the world. Now I am going for a ride. Good-bye."

3
Boo's Book

"It's gone!" Boo yelled in the library. "It's gone! *It's gone!*" Boo yelled louder this time.

Sammy went over to Boo. "What is gone, Boo?" he asked.

"*The Happy Dinosaur* is gone. It is always right there. And now it's *gone!*"

"Someone must have checked it out," Sammy said. "Get another book."

"I don't want another book. I want *my* book. Mine, mine, mine, mine, *mine*."

"Boo, it is not *your* book," Sammy said. "It belongs to the library."

"No, it is *mine*. I love that book. It's about a dinosaur, like *mine*. And he was lonely, like *mine*. And he found a girl, like *me*. Then he was not lonely anymore."

Boo went up to the desk. She said, "Someone took my book."

"What book?" the man at the desk asked.

"*The Happy Dinosaur.* See, I have a dinosaur and I promised to read it to him."

"Never break a promise to a dinosaur," the man said. "Wait, is this the book?"

"Yes! Yes! Yes!"

"Someone just turned it in." He gave Boo the book.

Boo hugged her book.

As Boo and Sammy left the library, she waved the book in the air so her dinosaur could see it. "I got it! I got it!" she called.

She turned to her brother. "Did you hear that?" she asked.

"What?"

"That rumbling. That's what dinosaurs do when they are happy. It says so in the book."

4

Boo Jumps on the Bed

"Stop jumping on the bed, Boo," Sammy said. "Dad told us not to jump on the bed."

"I have to jump on the bed," Boo said.

"Why, Boo?"

"It's the only way my dinosaur can see me," Boo said. "My dinosaur gets lonely without me. But I cannot jump high enough. Will you jump with me? Please, please, please, please, *please*."

"Oh, all right," Sammy said.

They jumped once. They jumped twice.

"He sees me! He sees me!" Boo said.

Dad's voice called, "Are you kids jumping on the bed again? I told you not to jump on the bed."

"We had to, Dad," Boo said. "My dinosaur gets lonely. He likes to see me."

Dad said, "If I hear any more about dinosaurs—"

"You won't, Dad," Sammy said quickly.

Dad said, "If I hear any more jumping on the bed—"

"You won't, Dad," they said together.

"Then, good night, kids."

"Good night, Dad!"

"Good night, Dinosaur," Boo whispered.

5
Boo High up a Tree

"Boo!" Sammy called.
 No answer.
 "Boo, supper's ready."
 No answer.
 "BOOOOOO!"
 "What?"
 Sammy looked up. Boo was high up in a tree.

"What are you doing?" Sammy asked.
"I'm waiting for my dinosaur," Boo said.
"Yeah, right."
"My dinosaur put me up here, and I need him to get me down."

Her brother sighed. "I'll get a ladder," he said. He went in the house and got a ladder.

When he came back, Boo was down from the tree. She was calling, "Good-bye! Good-bye!"

"I know, I know," Sammy said. "Your dinosaur came back, and you slid down his neck."

"How did you know?" Boo asked.

Then her face got sad. "Oh, I have bad news."

"What?" her brother asked.

"My dinosaur is going away. That's why I was saying good-bye."

"I'm not sorry to see him go," Sammy said. Then he stopped. "One time, long ago," he said, "I had a monkey friend named Peanut."

"You *did?*" Boo said.

"Yes, I did," Sammy said, "and I was very sorry when he went away."

"So you *know* how I feel," Boo said.

"I know," said Sammy.

6

Boo and the Magic Cape

"Boo, why do you have a towel tied around your neck?" Sammy asked. He and Boo were in the park.

Boo said, "It is not a towel. It is a magic cape."

"It looks like a towel," Sammy said.

"My dinosaur gave this to me before

he left. It is a magic cape. When I wear it, I can fly."

"I would like to see that," Sammy said. "Fly over to that tree."

Boo said, "The magic cape won't work if anyone is looking. You have to turn around."

Sammy turned around. He heard Boo running.

Then Boo said, "You can look now. I am at the tree."

Sammy looked. "Yes, you are at the tree," he said, "but you did not fly, you ran. I heard you."

Boo said, "I had to run to get started. Now I will fly to the corner, but you have to turn around."

"I am tired of this," Sammy said. "I am not going to turn around. I am going home."

When Sammy got home, Boo was waiting for him. She was sitting on the steps.

Sammy was surprised.

"Boo!" he said. "How did you get home so fast? Did you run all the way?"

Boo said, "No."

"Did you ride your dinosaur?" he asked.

"I did not ride my dinosaur," Boo said. "My dinosaur is gone."

"Then how did you get home so fast?" Sammy asked.

"You know," Boo said. "I flew."